Gr...
Garden

Dr. Monique Rodgers

Grandma's Garden

Dr. Monique Rodgers

United States of America

Published by Shooting Stars Publishing House 2024
Copyright © 2024 Dr. Monique Rodgers
All Rights Reserved.

ISBN:

Dedication

First, I want to give all the glory and thanks to God. His endless grace, love, and wisdom made this book a reality. Through every step of this journey, His presence has been my strength and inspiration, guiding me and blessing me beyond measure.

To my amazing grandmother, Mattie Rodgers—this book is for you. Your constant encouragement, faith, and love have been a foundation in my life. You've always believed in me, even when I didn't believe in myself. Your wisdom, kindness, and strength are qualities I admire deeply, and they've shaped who I am today. Thank you for teaching me the importance of prayer, perseverance, and trusting God no matter what.

To my mom, Apostle Genise Rodgers, I'm so grateful for your faith in me and your never-ending encouragement. Your prayers, love, and wisdom have been a steady light in my life. You've taught me how to stand strong in my purpose, and your belief in my dreams keeps me moving forward with confidence.

To my Mary Kay Director, Dawn, and Team Leader, Debbie, thank you for your incredible leadership and mentorship. Dawn, your ability to empower others has made a lasting impact on my life. Debbie, your positive energy and dedication inspire me daily. You both have shown me what it means to lead with authenticity, passion, and grace.

To my family and friends, thank you for always cheering me on. Your love and belief in me have been the support system I needed throughout this journey. Your encouragement has fueled my passion and kept me grounded during the highs and lows.

A special thank you to my editor and publishing team for your hard work, expertise, and attention to detail. Your efforts brought this book to life, and I'm so thankful for your partnership.

To my readers, thank you for joining me on this journey. My hope is that the words in these pages inspire, uplift, and remind you that you're capable of greatness. Keep walking your unique path with confidence and faith.

Lastly, this book is dedicated to everyone chasing big dreams, pushing through tough times, and believing in the power of transformation. May it remind you of the strength within you and the beauty of embracing your journey.

With love and gratitude,
Dr. Monique Rodgers

Contents

Dr. Monique Rodgers

Introduction

In the heart of a small southern town, nestled between rolling fields and shady oak trees, lies Grandma's garden—a sanctuary of beauty, life, and wisdom. For as long as I can remember, my grandmother, Maylena Robinson, has poured her heart and soul into that garden. It's more than a plot of land; it's a place of solace, healing, and connection. Every row of vegetables, every vine of ripened fruit, and every bloom of color tells a story of resilience, faith, and love.

Grandma Maylena isn't just a gardener of plants; she's a gardener of hearts. Her words of wisdom, grounded in scripture and life experience, have shaped generations. From her porch, where the scent of fresh-baked pies lingers, to the quiet rows of her garden where prayers are whispered under the sun, she's created a space where love grows as abundantly as her crops.

But even the strongest roots can be shaken. This year, the loss of her youngest son, Jex, to cancer brought a shadow to her vibrant life. Yet, in her grief, Grandma Maylena found comfort in her garden, leaning on her faith and the steady rhythm of planting and nurturing. It's here, surrounded by God's creation, that she finds the strength to keep moving forward and to inspire those around her.

This summer, one of her granddaughters, a successful author seeking direction and peace, comes to spend time with her. What starts as a visit turns into a season of transformation. Through the simplicity of weeding garden rows, sharing meals, and listening to Grandma Maylena's heartfelt prayers, lives are changed.

Dr. Monique Rodgers

Grandma's Garden is a story about faith, family, and the lessons we can learn from both nature and the people who love us unconditionally. It's about finding hope in the midst of loss, reconnecting with what truly matters, and understanding that every seed planted—whether in the soil or in the heart—has the potential to bloom into something beautiful.

As you turn these pages, I invite you into Grandma Maylena's world. May her story inspire you to cultivate your own garden of faith, love, and connection.

Welcome to *Grandma's Garden*. Let's grow together.

— **Dr. Monique Rodgers**

Chapter 1

The Garden of Healing

The morning sun spilled across the horizon, casting a golden glow over Maylena Robinson's garden. Dew clung to the leaves like tiny jewels, and the air smelled of damp earth and blooming jasmine. Maylena stood in the middle of it all, her hands wrapped around the handle of her favorite gardening hoe. This was her sacred space—a place where grief didn't feel so overwhelming and where hope quietly sprouted like the vegetables in her neatly arranged rows.

It had been three months since Jex passed, but the pain still hit her like a wave. He was her baby boy, the youngest of her six children, and his loss had left a void that no amount of casseroles, condolences, or

Dr. Monique Rodgers

Sunday sermons could fill. Yet, here in the garden, she felt his presence.

"Lord, give me strength," she whispered, her voice cracking as she knelt beside the tomato plants. Her fingers worked the soil gently, brushing against the roots as if she could coax the fruit to grow faster, fuller, stronger—anything to distract her from the ache in her heart.

The garden wasn't just a hobby; it was her sanctuary. Jex had always loved the garden, too. As a boy, he would trail behind her with his small watering can, laughing as he spilled more water on himself than the plants. "Mama, one day, I'm gonna grow the biggest watermelon this town's ever seen," he'd say with that wide, boyish grin.

Now, she tended the garden in his memory. Every row of vegetables and every blooming flower felt like a tribute to his life. She wiped a tear from her cheek, smearing a bit of dirt across her face. It didn't matter. Out here, appearances didn't count—only the work, the prayer, and the healing.

The magnolia tree at the back of the garden was her favorite spot. Its thick branches stretched wide like open arms, offering shade and solace. Maylena walked over to it, carrying her worn Bible and a mason jar of sweet tea. She settled onto the wooden bench beneath the tree, flipping through the pages until she found Psalm 34:18: *"The Lord is close to the brokenhearted and saves those who are crushed in spirit."*

She read the verse aloud, her voice steadying with each word. "You're close to me, Lord. I know You are."

Dr. Monique Rodgers

She closed her eyes and let the words settle deep into her soul.

As she sat there, the garden buzzed with life. Bees danced around the blossoms, a robin sang from the fencepost, and the wind whispered through the corn stalks. It was as if creation itself was reminding her that life goes on. Even in the midst of loss, there was still beauty to be found.

The screen door to her house creaked open, and Maylena's granddaughter Layla stepped out, waving. "Grandma! You out here praying again?"

Maylena smiled, waving her over. Layla was staying with her for the summer, and though she came seeking rest and inspiration for her next book, Maylena knew God had brought her here for something much deeper.

"Come on, child," Maylena called. "There's room for both of us under this tree."

Layla jogged over, her curly hair bouncing with each step. She plopped down on the bench beside her grandmother, glancing at the open Bible. "What are you reading today?"

"Psalm 34," Maylena said, handing her the book. "Go ahead and read it out loud."

Layla took the Bible, her voice soft as she read the verses. When she finished, she looked up at her grandmother, her brown eyes glistening. "That's beautiful. I needed that today."

"We all do," Maylena said, patting her hand. "The garden's good for that. It gives you space to think, to feel, and to hear from the Lord."

Dr. Monique Rodgers

They sat in silence for a moment, the kind of silence that doesn't need filling. Layla stared out at the garden, her mind turning. "Grandma, how do you do it? How do you keep going after losing Uncle Jex?"

Maylena exhaled, her gaze softening. "I come out here, I dig my hands in the dirt, and I talk to God. Some days I cry; some days I sing. And some days I just sit and listen. But I keep going because I know Jex wouldn't want me to stop. He'd want me to live, to grow, and to love—just like he did."

Layla nodded, wiping her own tears. "You're amazing, Grandma."

Maylena chuckled, the sound light and full of life. "I'm just a woman who loves her garden, her family, and her God. That's enough for me."

The two of them stayed there under the magnolia tree until the sun began to set, painting the sky in shades of pink and orange. The garden, now bathed in twilight, seemed to glow with a quiet magic. It wasn't just a patch of land; it was a place of healing, a place where faith and love grew strong roots.

And as Maylena stood to head inside, she looked back at the garden and whispered, "Thank You, Lord, for giving me this place and this moment. You're always good."

It was in that moment that she knew—healing wasn't about forgetting; it was about growing something beautiful in the midst of the pain.

Chapter 2:

Summer Plans

Alyssa Robinson stared out the car window as the familiar sight of her grandma Maylena's little house came into view. Nestled in the heart of a sleepy southern town, it was a world away from the bustling city she called home. The dusty gravel driveway crunched under the car tires as she pulled up. Her heart skipped a beat when she saw Maylena standing on the front porch, waving a handkerchief in one hand and balancing a pitcher of iced tea in the other.

Alyssa stepped out of the car, the sticky summer air wrapping around her like a blanket. "Grandma, you didn't have to go all out," she called, smiling despite herself.

"Baby, this isn't goin' all out. Wait 'til you see the pie coolin' in the kitchen," Maylena replied, her southern drawl as sweet as honey. She came down the steps with open arms, pulling Alyssa into a warm hug that felt like home.

Alyssa hadn't realized just how much she needed this—the peace, the familiarity, and the grounding presence of her grandmother. Life as a bestselling author had been a whirlwind. Book tours, interviews, deadlines—they'd all piled up, leaving her feeling stretched thin and disconnected from everything that truly mattered.

"It's been too long," Maylena said, holding her at arm's length to get a good look at her. "You look tired, girl. Busy life catchin' up with you?"

"You have no idea," Alyssa admitted with a sigh. "I needed to get away, and there's no better place than here."

"Well, come on inside. You can tell me all about it over some sweet tea and peach cobbler," Maylena said, grabbing one of Alyssa's bags and leading the way into the house.

The inside of the house was just as Alyssa remembered. The walls were lined with family photos—generations of Robinsons smiling down from every frame. The scent of fresh peaches and vanilla filled the air, and a gentle breeze floated through the open windows, carrying the sound of chirping cicadas.

"So," Maylena began as they settled at the kitchen table, "what made you finally take a break and come see your old grandma?"

Alyssa took a sip of tea, the cool sweetness a welcome relief from the heat. "Honestly, Grandma, I've been feeling... lost. My career is going great, but I feel like I've drifted from the things that matter—my family, my faith. And then I thought of you, out here in this peaceful little town, and I knew this was where I needed to be."

Maylena nodded, a knowing smile spreading across her face. "God has a funny way of bringing us back where we need to be, doesn't He? Sounds like you're here for more than just a break, though."

Alyssa looked down at her glass, her thoughts swirling. "Maybe I am. I guess I'm hoping to figure some things out this summer."

"Well, you've come to the right place," Maylena said. "This house and that garden out back have a way of workin' things out in a person's heart. But first, let's get you unpacked and settled."

Alyssa's Retreat

Over the next few days, Alyssa settled into a rhythm she hadn't known she needed. Mornings started with coffee on the porch, where Maylena read her Bible aloud, her voice steady and soothing. Alyssa often joined in, though she felt rusty—her faith had taken a backseat to her busy life for far too long.

"Why don't you come to church with me on Sunday?" Maylena asked one morning as they watered the garden together.

Alyssa hesitated. "I don't know, Grandma. I haven't been to church in years. I wouldn't even know what to do."

"Child, you just show up," Maylena said with a chuckle. "Let God handle the rest. Besides, everyone's gonna want to see you. They still talk about your book around here like you're some kind of celebrity."

The thought made Alyssa laugh. "Maybe I will, then. It'd be nice to see some familiar faces."

Lessons from the Garden

Each afternoon, Alyssa joined her grandmother in the garden. At first, she simply followed along, watching

Dr. Monique Rodgers

Maylena tend to the rows of tomatoes, cucumbers, and okra with a quiet reverence. But soon, she found herself digging in, quite literally.

"You know," Maylena said one day as they weeded a row of green beans, "this garden isn't just about growin' food. It's about life. You plant a seed, you water it, you tend to it, and God takes care of the rest. Same with your soul, Alyssa."

Alyssa looked up from the dirt, wiping her brow. "I guess I've been neglecting my 'garden,' haven't I?"

"We all do sometimes," Maylena replied. "But it's never too late to start again."

Those words stuck with Alyssa. Each day, as she worked alongside her grandmother, she began to feel the tiniest bit of that lost connection returning—like a seed starting to sprout.

The Dinner Table

Evenings were spent around the dinner table, piled high with fresh dishes straight from the garden. Cornbread, fried okra, tomato salad—it was a feast of simple, wholesome food that nourished more than just the body.

Maylena always led the family in prayer before the meal, her words heartfelt and genuine. "Thank You, Lord, for bringing Alyssa home for the summer. Thank You for this food and the hands that prepared it. Bless this time together and guide us in all that we do. Amen."

Sitting there, surrounded by love and laughter, Alyssa felt something she hadn't felt in a long time—peace.

A Summer of Rediscovery

Dr. Monique Rodgers

By the end of the first week, Alyssa realized her summer at Grandma Maylena's was shaping up to be more than just a break from the chaos of her career. It was a chance to reconnect—with her family, her faith, and herself.

As she lay in bed that night, listening to the crickets sing outside her window, Alyssa whispered a simple prayer. "Thank You, God, for bringing me here. Help me make the most of this time."

She didn't know what the rest of the summer would hold, but for the first time in years, she felt like she was exactly where she needed to be.

Chapter 3:

Early Mornings and Bible Time

The smell of something warm and buttery pulled Alyssa from a dreamless sleep. She blinked against the morning light streaming through the thin curtains and stretched lazily. It took her a second to remember where she was—Grandma Maylena's house, where mornings seemed to wake up slower, quieter.

The faint sound of singing floated up the stairs. Alyssa recognized the hymn immediately: *"Great Is Thy Faithfulness."* Grandma's rich alto carried through the house, full of the kind of joy and peace that made you stop and listen.

Alyssa slipped out of bed, pulling on a robe before heading down the hall. The smell of fresh biscuits grew stronger as she reached the kitchen, where Maylena stood by the stove, humming as she flipped sizzling sausage patties in a cast-iron skillet.

"Good morning, sleepyhead!" Maylena greeted without turning around. "I was wonderin' when you'd join me. Breakfast is just about ready."

"Morning, Grandma," Alyssa replied, yawning as she slid into one of the chairs at the kitchen table. A Bible lay open in front of Maylena's spot, next to a steaming mug of tea.

"You're always up so early," Alyssa said, marveling at her grandmother's energy.

"Old habits," Maylena said with a chuckle, setting a plate of biscuits and sausage on the table. "The Lord and I have a standing appointment every morning. Wouldn't want to miss it."

Alyssa glanced at the Bible, its pages well-worn and full of handwritten notes. "You do this every day?"

"Every single day," Maylena said, pouring herself a fresh cup of tea. "It's how I stay grounded. Life has a way of throwing things at you, and if you don't stay rooted in the Word, you'll find yourself blown every which way."

Alyssa nodded but didn't say anything. She couldn't remember the last time she'd opened a Bible, let alone sat down to really read it.

A Morning Routine with Purpose

As they ate, Maylena shared her routine. She started every day with prayer, asking God for guidance and strength. Then she read a passage from her Bible, jotting down thoughts or prayers in the margins.

"This here's one of my favorite verses," she said, tapping the page with a finger. "'The Lord is near to the brokenhearted and saves the crushed in spirit'—Psalm 34:18. That verse carried me through when Jex passed. I'd read it every morning, and it felt like God was whisperin' it straight to my heart."

Alyssa looked down at her plate, her appetite suddenly gone. She hadn't really talked to Grandma about Jex's death, not in any meaningful way. It had been too painful, too raw.

"I don't know how you do it," Alyssa admitted softly. "How you keep going after losing him."

Maylena reached across the table and took Alyssa's hand, her grip warm and steady. "I don't do it on my own, baby. The good Lord gives me the strength. I miss Jex every single day, but I know he's with Jesus, and that gives me peace."

Alyssa blinked back tears, her throat tightening. She envied her grandmother's faith, her unwavering trust in something bigger than herself.

Tea and Scriptures

After breakfast, they lingered at the table, sipping tea as Maylena turned to another passage.

"Listen to this," she said, her voice steady. "'Come to me, all who labor and are heavy laden, and I will give you rest. Take my yoke upon you, and learn from me, for I am gentle and lowly in heart, and you will find rest for your souls'—Matthew 11:28-29. You've been carryin' a heavy load, haven't you, Alyssa?"

Alyssa hesitated but nodded. "I guess I have. Work, life—it all feels like too much sometimes."

"Well, there's your answer right there," Maylena said, pointing to the passage. "You've got to lay it all down at His feet. Let Him carry what you can't."

Alyssa sighed, feeling the weight of those words. Could it really be that simple? She'd spent so much time trying to control everything, to make sure every piece of her life fit perfectly. Maybe it was time to let go a little.

Finding Strength in Faith

Over the next few mornings, Alyssa joined Maylena for her Bible time. At first, she mostly listened, letting the words wash over her. But soon, she found herself asking questions, scribbling notes in the margins of an old Bible Maylena had given her.

"What does this mean?" Alyssa asked one morning, holding up the verse Maylena had read from Matthew.

"It means you don't have to do it all by yourself," Maylena explained. "God's not askin' you to be perfect. He's askin' you to trust Him. Big difference."

Alyssa nodded, her heart beginning to soften. She hadn't realized how much she needed this time, this space to reconnect—not just with her grandmother, but with her faith.

A New Perspective

One morning, as they sat beneath the magnolia tree with their Bibles in their laps, Alyssa turned to her grandmother. "How do you keep your faith so strong?"

Maylena smiled, her eyes full of wisdom. "Faith isn't about feelin' strong, baby. It's about leanin' on God when you're not. It's about rememberin' that He's faithful, even when life doesn't make sense."

Alyssa looked out at the garden, its rows of vegetables glistening with dew in the morning sun. She thought about everything her grandmother had been through, about the quiet strength that radiated from her.

"I think I want to try," Alyssa said finally. "To have what you have."

Maylena reached over and patted her hand. "You're already on your way, sweetheart. Just take it one day at a time."

As the days passed, Alyssa found herself looking forward to these early mornings. They became a source of peace, a chance to reset and reflect. And slowly, she began to feel a shift—like a seed planted deep within her was finally starting to grow.

Chapter 4:

Lessons from the Soil

The morning sun bathed the garden in a warm, golden glow as Maylena Robinson adjusted her wide-brimmed straw hat. She held out a pair of gloves and a basket to Alyssa, who stood at the garden gate, looking slightly out of place in her designer sneakers and yoga pants.

"Come on, girl, you're not gonna learn standin' there," Maylena teased, motioning Alyssa over with a wave of her hand.

Alyssa chuckled, slipping on the gloves. "I'm not sure I'm cut out for this, Grandma. The closest I've come to gardening is watering the ficus in my apartment."

Maylena laughed, her warm, throaty chuckle filling the air. "Well, today's the day you learn. Grab that basket, and let's start with the tomatoes. They're callin' for some attention."

The Language of the Garden

The garden was alive with color and sound: rows of leafy greens, climbing vines heavy with cucumbers, and the soft buzz of bees flitting from flower to flower. Maylena crouched beside a tomato plant, her hands deftly picking bright red fruit.

"See these leaves here?" she said, pointing to some that were starting to yellow. "They've done their job, but now they're takin' up energy the plant needs for the fruit. You've got to know when to let go of what's no longer helpin' you grow."

Alyssa nodded, her gloved hands carefully following her grandmother's instructions. "So, pruning is like... life?"

"Exactly," Maylena said with a knowing smile. "Life's full of things that served a purpose for a season, but when the time comes, you've got to let them go to make room for new growth. Same goes for faith. You can't hold onto fear and trust God at the same time."

Seeds of Wisdom

As they worked their way down the rows, Maylena shared more of her wisdom, her voice steady and sure. "Life is like a garden," she said, pulling a cucumber from its vine and dropping it into the basket. "You plant seeds, you nurture them, and you wait. Sometimes storms come and try to tear it all apart, but you trust that God will bring the harvest in His time."

Alyssa paused, brushing dirt off her hands. "What if the storm's too strong? What if it ruins everything?"

Maylena leaned on her trowel, looking her granddaughter square in the eye. "Then you replant, baby. You start over. Life's not about how many times you fall; it's about how many times you get back up and keep planting. God's faithful like that. He don't leave you in the storm—He walks with you through it."

Alyssa felt a lump in her throat. She thought about her own storms—the heartbreak, the pressure of success, and the doubts that kept her up at night. Somehow, standing here in this garden, her grandmother's words felt like water to her parched soul.

Journaling the Lessons

Later that evening, after washing up and sharing a hearty lunch of cucumber salad and fresh tomato sandwiches, Alyssa sat on the porch swing with a notebook in her lap.

She had started jotting down bits and pieces of their conversations, snippets of Maylena's wisdom that stuck with her. "Prune what doesn't serve you." "Trust God through the storm." "The harvest is worth the wait." Each line felt like a treasure, a nugget of truth that might help someone else as much as it was helping her.

"Whatcha writin', honey?" Maylena asked, stepping onto the porch with two glasses of sweet tea.

Alyssa smiled and shrugged. "Just some things you've said today. I don't want to forget them."

Maylena handed her a glass and sat beside her. "Good. The Lord gives us wisdom to share, not to keep to ourselves. You never know who might need to hear it."

Alyssa nodded, a thought forming in the back of her mind. What if these lessons, this time with Grandma, could be more than just personal growth? What if it could be a way to reach others, to inspire them the way Maylena was inspiring her?

The Power of Perseverance

The next day, they returned to the garden, this time tackling the weeds threatening to choke the squash plants.

"These things are stubborn," Alyssa said, tugging at a particularly deep-rooted one.

"That they are," Maylena agreed, kneeling beside her. "But you can't let 'em take over. Weeds are like doubt and fear—they creep in when you're not lookin' and try to steal your joy. You've got to pull them out by the root."

Alyssa sat back on her heels, sweat beading on her forehead. "Does it ever get easier?"

Maylena smiled, wiping her hands on her apron. "Not always, but it gets worth it. Perseverance builds character, and character builds hope. That's straight from Romans 5:3-4, baby. And hope? That's somethin' no weed can take from you."

A Growing Connection

By the end of the week, Alyssa's hands were sore, her back ached, and her sneakers were permanently stained with dirt. But she didn't mind. She felt closer to her grandmother than she ever had, and more importantly, she felt a stirring in her own heart—a sense of peace and purpose she hadn't known she was missing.

As they stood at the garden gate, baskets full of fresh vegetables, Maylena looked at Alyssa with pride.

"You're catchin' on, girl," she said, patting her on the back.

"I've got a good teacher," Alyssa replied with a grin.

Maylena laughed. "And you've got good soil. The Lord's planted somethin' in you, Alyssa. I can see it. You just keep waterin' it with faith and hard work, and you'll see the harvest."

Dr. Monique Rodgers

Alyssa nodded, her heart full. For the first time in a long time, she felt like she was exactly where she was meant to be—standing in her grandmother's garden, learning lessons she didn't even know she needed.

Chapter 5:

Meals That Heal

The smell of fresh cornbread baking in the oven filled Maylena's kitchen, mingling with the earthy aroma of collard greens simmering on the stove. Alyssa stood at the counter, trying to chop onions without crying. Grandma Maylena, ever the expert, moved gracefully between pots and pans, humming an old hymn.

"You're cuttin' too slow, baby," Maylena teased, glancing over her shoulder. "That onion's not gonna chop itself."

Alyssa laughed, wiping her eyes. "I don't know how you do this without tears, Grandma. It's like this onion knows all my secrets."

Maylena chuckled and handed her a dish towel. "Well, the trick is to keep your heart open but your hands steady. Cooking's like life—messy sometimes, but always worth the effort."

Jex's Favorites

"Now," Maylena said, stirring the pot of greens, "these collards were Jex's favorite. Lord, that boy could eat a whole pot by himself if I let him. He'd always say, 'Mama, ain't nobody cook greens like you.'"

Alyssa smiled, touched by the warmth in her grandmother's voice. "He had good taste. What's the secret, though? These are better than any I've ever had."

Maylena winked. "It's all about love. You gotta season with care and give it time to cook down just right. Life's like that too—everything good takes patience."

Alyssa nodded, jotting down notes in the little journal she'd started keeping since her arrival. She wanted to remember these moments, these lessons, and maybe even share them one day.

Cooking as a Bond

As the meal came together, the kitchen turned into a symphony of clinking pots, sizzling pans, and shared laughter. Maylena showed Alyssa how to knead dough for cornbread and mix the perfect sweet tea.

"Cooking's more than just puttin' food on the table," Maylena said. "It's about connection. When we cook, we're sharing pieces of ourselves—our time, our love, our stories."

Alyssa looked up from her task, moved by her grandmother's words. "I never thought about it that way. I guess I've been so busy, I forgot what it's like to slow down and just... enjoy this."

"Well, that's why you're here, ain't it?" Maylena said with a grin. "To remember what really matters."

Dinner with the Family

By the time dinner was ready, the small dining room was alive with chatter. Alyssa's cousins, aunts, and uncles filled the seats, their laughter echoing off the walls. The table was a feast of fresh garden vegetables, crispy fried chicken, buttery cornbread, and, of course, the collard greens that had been Jex's favorite.

Maylena stood at the head of the table, her presence commanding yet comforting. "Before we eat, let's bow our heads and thank the Lord for this meal and the hands that prepared it."

The room fell silent as she led the prayer, her words rich with gratitude and love. Alyssa felt a lump in her throat as she joined in the chorus of "Amen."

As they ate, the conversation flowed easily, stories weaving together like a tapestry. Maylena shared memories of Jex, her eyes sparkling with both sorrow and joy.

"Jex loved this table," she said. "He always said it didn't matter how hard life got, as long as we had each other and a good meal to share."

The Healing Power of Community

As the evening went on, Alyssa noticed how the simple act of eating together brought everyone closer. People laughed, shared stories, and even shed a few tears. It was as if the table itself was a place of healing, a space where everyone could feel seen and loved.

After dinner, Alyssa found herself sitting on the porch with her grandmother, the cool night air wrapping around them.

"You see what I mean now?" Maylena asked, rocking gently in her chair.

"About what?" Alyssa said, sipping her tea.

"About the power of breaking bread together. A meal's not just food—it's an offering. It's a way to show love, to heal wounds, to remind each other that we're not alone."

Alyssa nodded, her heart full. "I think I'm starting to get it, Grandma. It's more than just cooking; it's about creating something that brings people together."

Maylena smiled, reaching over to pat her hand. "That's right, baby. And if you can carry that with you, no matter where you go, you'll always have a little piece of home."

A Seed Planted

Later that night, as Alyssa wrote in her journal, she realized how much her grandmother's wisdom was changing her. She wasn't just learning how to cook; she was learning how to slow down, how to connect, how to heal.

She thought about Jex and how much he had loved this family, this table, this life. She felt a sense of responsibility to carry that legacy forward, to make sure these lessons didn't stop with her.

Dr. Monique Rodgers

The last thing she wrote before closing her journal was a single sentence: *"Meals that heal are made with love."*

And with that, she knew she was starting to find her way back to what truly mattered.

Chapter 6:

The Storm

The air had grown heavy as the late afternoon sun began to dip behind the trees. Alyssa, who had been sitting on the porch with her journal, felt the first drop of rain hit her arm. She glanced up at the sky—dark, swirling clouds were rolling in from the west, and the wind picked up suddenly, sending leaves swirling around the yard.

"Grandma," Alyssa called out, her voice rising in concern, "It looks like a storm's coming."

Maylena stood at the kitchen window, peering out at the rapidly changing sky. Her face remained calm, but Alyssa could see a slight crease between her grandmother's brows.

"Yes, it's coming fast. We need to get to the garden," Maylena said, her tone steady. "Grab your shoes, and let's move quickly."

Alyssa, though still unfamiliar with how unpredictable the southern weather could be, didn't hesitate. She slipped into her sneakers and followed Maylena out the door.

The Garden in the Storm

The moment they stepped into the yard, the storm hit with a vengeance. The wind howled, and the rain started coming down in sheets. Maylena and Alyssa sprinted toward the garden, the wild wind whipping their clothes and soaking them in an instant.

"Quick, we need to get to the tomatoes and cucumbers before the wind knocks them over!" Maylena shouted above the roar of the storm.

Alyssa struggled to keep up, feeling the rain beat against her face and the ground shift beneath her feet. But there was no time to waste.

Maylena reached the tomato vines first, her hands moving quickly to gather the ripe fruits. She worked with a focus and intensity that Alyssa had never seen from her before. As the storm raged on, the sound of the rain drowned out everything else, but Maylena's voice was steady as she called to Alyssa.

"Get the cucumbers and peppers, baby! We'll save what we can."

Alyssa nodded and rushed over to the cucumber patch, fighting the wind as she carefully picked the vegetables, placing them in a basket. She tried to ignore the sting of the rain as it hit her skin, but the urgency of the situation made her work faster.

"Are you sure we can save everything?" Alyssa shouted to her grandmother, her voice nearly drowned out by the storm.

Maylena didn't pause in her task, her hands moving like clockwork. She was determined, even as the storm showed no signs of letting up.

"Do the best we can, Alyssa. We're not in control of the storm, but we can control how we respond to it. Trust God, baby," Maylena called back, her voice calm and full of conviction.

A Calm in the Chaos

Alyssa didn't quite understand how her grandmother could remain so composed. She herself felt the storm's power, the way the earth seemed to shake under its intensity. The wind blew harder, and the rain fell in torrents, soaking her through. But Maylena remained at the center of the garden, as if the storm was a mere inconvenience.

"Grandma, how do you stay so calm?" Alyssa shouted over the storm, dropping another cucumber into her basket.

Maylena straightened, wiping the rain from her face with the back of her hand. She looked at Alyssa with eyes that seemed to see something beyond the chaos around them.

"Psalm 46:1," Maylena said softly, her voice steady despite the storm's fury. "God is our refuge and strength, a very present help in trouble."

Alyssa blinked, her hands momentarily still. She hadn't expected that response, but hearing the verse from her grandmother, it was like a wave of peace washed over her.

"You really believe that, don't you?" Alyssa asked, her voice quieter now, the storm not seeming as overwhelming as before.

Maylena gave her a look that was both knowing and kind. "Baby, you have to believe it. In life, you'll face storms—literal and figurative. And you can't control the storms, but you can control how you respond to them. We can choose to trust in God's presence, even when the wind is howling and the rain is pouring."

Alyssa felt something stir inside her, a deep desire to believe in that kind of peace, that kind of trust. She had been so focused on her own worries—her career, her doubts about her faith, the disconnection she felt from her family—but in this moment, under the shelter of her grandmother's calm presence, the world seemed to slow down.

"Let's finish this," Maylena said, reaching for another handful of tomatoes. "There's always work to do, even in the storm."

The Aftermath

The storm seemed to last forever, but eventually, the rain began to taper off, and the wind died down. As suddenly as it had appeared, the storm was gone, leaving behind a stillness in the air.

Maylena and Alyssa stood in the garden, drenched but determined. The ground was muddy, and the plants were bent, but the vegetables they had salvaged were safe.

"Look at the damage," Alyssa murmured, surveying the garden. Some of the plants had been flattened, others were broken, but the majority of the harvest had been saved.

"Not everything is going to survive, baby. But what we've salvaged is enough for today," Maylena said, her voice low but strong. "That's how life is. Sometimes, storms come, and we lose things we can't get back. But God's mercy is new every day. We trust that He will provide."

Alyssa wiped the rain from her face and nodded, the weight of her grandmother's words settling in her heart. She looked down at the tomatoes and cucumbers in her basket, suddenly aware of the significance of the moment.

Maylena smiled, reaching out to touch Alyssa's shoulder. "You're learning, I can see it. The storms don't last forever. And neither does the damage. After a storm, the sun always comes out again."

Alyssa breathed deeply, taking in the fresh, damp air. She could feel the tension in her chest loosen, as though the storm outside had washed away some of the worries that had weighed her down for so long.

"Thank you, Grandma," Alyssa said softly. "I don't know if I could've made it through that storm without you."

Maylena chuckled and winked. "You didn't make it through alone. You've got God with you every step of the way, just like I do. Now, let's go inside and have some of that cornbread we made earlier. You've earned it."

As they walked back toward the house, Alyssa looked at the sky, which had started to clear. The storm had

Dr. Monique Rodgers

passed, and the sun was breaking through the clouds, casting a soft golden light over the garden.

She felt a peace inside her—a peace that, like the sun after the storm, had been there all along, waiting for her to trust in it.

Chapter 7:

Church on Sunday

The sun had just begun to peek over the horizon as Alyssa sat on the porch, sipping her coffee and watching the morning mist rise off the fields. There was a stillness in the air, the kind of peaceful calm that always seemed to follow a storm. It had been an exhausting week—one filled with long conversations with Grandma Maylena, hours of journaling, and reflections on the grief she had been carrying ever since her uncle Jex had passed away.

Her thoughts were interrupted when she heard Maylena's familiar voice calling from the door.

"Alyssa, it's time to get ready for church!"

Dr. Monique Rodgers

Alyssa looked up at her grandmother, who was standing in the doorway with a warm smile on her face. There was something about Maylena that made even the most routine things feel sacred, as if every moment was infused with purpose.

"Church?" Alyssa asked, still groggy from a late night of writing.

"Yes, darling. It's Sunday, and we're going to church. You're coming with me, aren't you?" Maylena's voice was full of gentle encouragement.

Alyssa hesitated. It wasn't that she didn't want to go—it was more the fact that she hadn't been to church in years. Between her book tours, deadlines, and the whirlwind of her career, the idea of sitting in a pew surrounded by strangers seemed like a distant memory. She hadn't been close to her faith for a long time, and part of her wasn't sure if she was ready to face it again.

But looking at her grandmother, Alyssa could see the love and warmth radiating from her, and she knew that if there was ever a time to start reconnecting with her faith, it was now.

"Okay, Grandma. I'll go," Alyssa said, setting her coffee cup down and standing up to join her.

The Church in the Country

The church wasn't far from Maylena's house—a small, charming building nestled on the outskirts of town. It was the kind of church that felt like a second home, with its white wooden exterior and steeple that reached toward the sky. Alyssa could see the congregation already gathered on the front steps, chatting and laughing in the warm sunlight.

As they walked toward the door, Alyssa felt a mixture of emotions—nervousness, curiosity, and a deep sense of longing she hadn't quite acknowledged before. She had been so disconnected from her family, her faith, and even from herself that it felt like stepping into a different world.

But as soon as they entered the church, something shifted. The smell of wood, the soft murmur of voices, and the familiar hum of a gospel hymn being played on the piano instantly put her at ease. People turned to greet Maylena with open arms and warm smiles, calling out her name and embracing her like family.

"This is Alyssa, my granddaughter," Maylena introduced her, her voice full of pride. "She's visiting for the summer."

Alyssa gave a small wave and offered a hesitant smile. To her surprise, the congregation welcomed her with open arms, as if she had always been a part of their community.

"Come, sit with us," an older woman named Miss Edna said, taking Alyssa's hand and guiding her to a seat. "We've been praying for you."

Alyssa blinked in surprise. She didn't know these people, but the warmth they offered was undeniable. It was like they could see something in her that she couldn't yet recognize in herself—a sense of worth, of belonging, that she had been missing for far too long.

Dr. Monique Rodgers

The Sermon That Spoke to Her

The service began with a few hymns and a prayer, and then Pastor Samuel, the elderly but energetic preacher, took the pulpit. His presence was commanding, but there was a softness in his voice that immediately put Alyssa at ease.

The topic for the day was "Letting Go and Trusting God." Alyssa didn't know why, but those words hit her like a freight train. She had spent so many years holding on to her career, her success, and her grief over Jex's death. She had buried her emotions deep, refusing to face them, hoping that writing and busyness would somehow fill the void.

But as Pastor Samuel spoke, Alyssa felt the weight of his words in her chest.

"Sometimes," Pastor Samuel said, his voice softening, "we carry burdens that we were never meant to bear. We hold on to grief, to unforgiveness, to past pain, and we wonder why we feel so exhausted. The truth is, when we try to carry these things ourselves, we're only making the load heavier. God doesn't ask us to carry our burdens alone."

Alyssa's breath caught in her throat. She wasn't the only one struggling. Everyone around her seemed to be feeling it, too. The room felt alive with energy, as if the words were connecting with something deep inside each person, including her.

Pastor Samuel continued, "Letting go isn't about forgetting. It's about trusting that God will carry us through our darkest moments. It's about surrendering the things that are too heavy for us to carry on our own, and allowing God to heal us from the inside out."

Alyssa closed her eyes, letting the words wash over her. She thought about Jex—the way she had never fully processed his death, how she had buried her grief behind the walls of her career. She had been so consumed with success that she had neglected the things that truly mattered. She had neglected her heart.

"You don't have to hold on to everything, my friends," Pastor Samuel said with a knowing smile. "You can trust God to carry the weight. You can let go of the pain, the fear, the guilt, and trust that He will make a way for you."

Alyssa's heart pounded in her chest. For the first time in years, she felt the walls inside her begin to crack.

The grief that had been sitting there for so long—unresolved and heavy—began to move within her. It wasn't gone, but she could feel that God was inviting her to let go of it.

A Moment of Healing

As the sermon ended and the congregation stood to sing the final hymn, Alyssa felt a lump in her throat. She had always been afraid to face her emotions, to let go of the pain she had carried for so long. But now, surrounded by these people who had accepted her without question, something inside her shifted.

She stood there, quietly singing along, her voice trembling slightly, but she felt a warmth spread through her chest. Maylena stood beside her, singing with her hands raised in worship, her face full of peace. Alyssa looked at her grandmother, amazed at her unwavering faith, and felt a deep sense of gratitude.

As the service came to an end, Pastor Samuel approached Maylena and Alyssa. "It's so good to have you back with us, Maylena," he said with a smile. "And Alyssa, I hope today's message touched your heart. Remember, you don't have to carry everything on your own."

Alyssa smiled, the weight in her chest feeling lighter than it had in years. "Thank you," she said softly, her voice filled with emotion. "It really did."

A New Beginning

As they walked out of the church and into the bright sunlight, Alyssa felt different. She didn't have all the answers yet, but something had changed. She had heard the message she needed to hear, and for the first time in a long time, she felt like she could let go of the grief that had been holding her back. She could trust God to carry her through the struggles, just as He had carried Maylena through her own losses.

Alyssa took a deep breath and looked up at the sky, feeling a renewed sense of hope. She wasn't sure where this journey would take her, but she was ready to take the next step. And she knew that, no matter what, she wasn't alone.

Chapter 8:

Seeds of Legacy

The sun was beginning to dip behind the trees, casting long shadows over Maylena's garden. The air was thick with the scent of fresh earth and the hum of cicadas, a perfect evening for planting. Alyssa stood beside her grandmother, her hands gripping the small garden trowel, and watched as Maylena expertly dug into the soil, preparing the earth for the new seeds.

"Grandma, are you sure you want to plant this late?" Alyssa asked, looking at the sky, which was turning soft shades of pink and orange.

Maylena smiled, wiping a thin layer of sweat from her brow. "The best time to plant is when the soil is warm, and the evening is calm. Don't worry about the timing. God's timing is always perfect."

Alyssa nodded, glancing over the rows of vegetables already growing in the garden—tomatoes, cucumbers, collard greens—all planted with care. The garden had become a metaphor for her life over the past few weeks, and now, as they bent over the soil together, it felt as though a deeper lesson was about to unfold.

As Maylena handed her a small packet of seeds, Alyssa couldn't help but ask, "Grandma, what's your secret to a garden like this? You've got the greenest thumb I've ever seen."

Maylena chuckled, her voice warm and full of wisdom. "Well, I've spent a lot of years working this soil. But the real secret is not just in planting—it's in believing that the seeds will grow. It's the same with life. You plant seeds in your heart, in your

Dr. Monique Rodgers

relationships, in your faith, and then you trust that God will make them bloom."

Alyssa gently pressed the seeds into the soil, her fingers moving with a newfound sense of purpose. As she did, she felt the weight of her grandmother's words settle in her chest. There was something powerful in that simple act of planting—not just the seeds, but the faith behind them.

For a moment, there was a comfortable silence between them as they worked. The rhythmic sound of trowels digging into the earth was the only noise, apart from the occasional bird call and the gentle rustle of leaves. But then, Maylena broke the silence, her voice steady but full of emotion.

"I didn't always have it easy, you know." Maylena paused, looking out over the garden, as though the plants themselves might give her strength to continue.

Alyssa stopped, her hand still in the soil, and turned her attention fully to her grandmother. "What do you mean?"

Maylena sighed, a long, slow breath that seemed to carry the weight of years. "When I was young, I didn't have much. I didn't have the garden, the house, the family I have now. I had to work hard for everything I've built, and I had to learn how to trust God in ways I never imagined."

She paused again, her hands resting on her hips as she looked up at the sky. "I raised three children on my own after their father left us. Life wasn't easy. There were days when I didn't know how I was going to make ends meet, but I always prayed, always trusted that God would provide."

Alyssa felt a pang of guilt, her own life feeling so different from her grandmother's. She had grown up in a world of opportunities—book deals, interviews, and luxury—but she had never really considered the struggles her grandmother had faced. She had never truly understood the depth of her grandmother's faith, how much Maylena had relied on God to get through the tough times.

"Grandma, that must have been so hard," Alyssa said, her voice softer now, a mix of admiration and sympathy.

Maylena smiled, but there was a quiet sadness in her eyes. "It was. But God was always there. He sent people to help, and He provided when I didn't think it was possible. And through it all, I never gave up on my faith." She looked at Alyssa, her eyes piercing through the evening light. "The hardest part, Alyssa, was not just raising my children—it was leaving a legacy. I wanted them to know that no matter what, they could trust God, that He would always make a way for them. I wanted them to grow up knowing what it meant to stand firm in faith, even when the world around us was shaking."

Alyssa felt a lump form in her throat. She had always known her grandmother was strong, but hearing the details of her struggles, her sacrifices, and her unshakable faith made her heart swell with pride. Maylena had built her family on the foundation of faith, and it was something that Alyssa had only recently started to understand.

As Maylena continued to plant the seeds, she glanced at Alyssa again. "Everyone has a legacy, you know. We all leave something behind. It might be the way we love our children, the work we do, or the faith we pass on. But what matters is that we plant seeds that will grow long after we're gone. That's the kind of legacy I want to leave."

Alyssa thought about those words for a moment. She had spent so much time focused on building her career—on writing books and going on tours—but had she been planting the right seeds? Had she been thinking about the legacy she wanted to leave behind?

Without realizing it, she had already started planting the seeds of her own legacy in the garden of her family's faith. But there was something more she could do. Something more she needed to do.

"I think I know what I want to do next," Alyssa said, her voice quiet but determined. "I want to write a book—one that honors your legacy, Grandma. I want to share your story, your faith, everything you've taught me about trusting God. It's time I plant those seeds in the world."

Maylena's face lit up with a proud smile. "Alyssa, I think that's a beautiful idea." She reached out and squeezed her granddaughter's hand. "If you can inspire even one person to trust God and hold on to their faith, then you've planted a mighty seed."

Alyssa's heart felt full as she continued working alongside her grandmother. In that moment, she realized that writing this book wouldn't just be a tribute to Maylena—it would be a tribute to the legacy of faith that had shaped their family, a legacy that would continue to grow, generation after generation.

As the sun finally set, casting its final rays over the garden, Alyssa felt something inside her shift. She wasn't just planting seeds in the soil anymore. She was planting seeds of hope, faith, and love that would grow into something much bigger than herself.

The seeds had been planted. Now, it was time to trust God to bring the harvest.

And she knew, deep in her heart, that He would.

Chapter 9:

The Family Gathering

Maylena's house buzzed with life. It wasn't just a home; it was the heart of the family, a gathering place for generations of stories, laughter, and love. The kitchen, as always, smelled of freshly baked cornbread and collard greens. The scent was so familiar to Alyssa that it felt like a warm embrace. Today, it wasn't just her and Grandma Maylena in the house—it was everyone. The Robinson family was gathering for their annual reunion, and the house was alive with the sounds of children running through the halls, cousins reconnecting, and the older generation exchanging stories and memories.

Alyssa had spent the last few weeks in the small southern town, taking time away from her hectic life in the city. The peaceful routine of working in the garden, attending church with Grandma, and cooking meals together had grounded her in ways she hadn't expected. But now, as the family trickled in, she realized how much more this family reunion was going to mean. It wasn't just a gathering—it was a celebration of what made them who they were.

The first to arrive was her cousin, Luke, with his wife, Tamara, and their two kids, Mia and Caleb. Alyssa watched as Luke stepped out of the truck, his broad shoulders and easy smile bringing a sense of relief to the moment. He walked up to Alyssa, gave her a big hug, and said, "Hey, cuz. It's been way too long."

"It really has!" Alyssa said, laughing. "How's Tamara? How's the crew?"

"Tamara's good," Luke replied, shaking his head. "You know, she's always on top of things. Caleb and Mia, they're growing like weeds. It's hard to keep up with them these days."

The laughter of the kids echoed through the house as Mia and Caleb dashed past them, chasing each other with wild abandon. The sound was like music to Alyssa's ears. The innocence of children's laughter always brought a sense of warmth and joy, and she could feel the weight of her recent struggles and worries begin to lift.

Her Uncle Marcus and Aunt Linda arrived next, bringing with them the smell of their famous barbecue sauce. Alyssa loved how Aunt Linda always brought something extra to the table—both literally and figuratively. She was the life of every party, always

Dr. Monique Rodgers

cracking jokes and keeping the energy high. Uncle Marcus, on the other hand, was a man of few words but immeasurable love. His hugs were tight, his handshake firm, and his presence calming. Together, they made the perfect pair.

"Look at you, Alyssa," Aunt Linda said, giving her a tight hug. "You've been missing out on these family gatherings! We've all been talking about how good it is to have you back."

"I'm glad to be back," Alyssa replied, a little caught off guard by the warmth of their welcome. "I needed this. You guys are exactly what I needed."

Uncle Marcus smiled quietly from behind her aunt. "Well, don't be a stranger next time."

Alyssa couldn't help but smile. It felt like she was home again.

As the afternoon went on, more and more family members trickled in. Her cousins, great-aunts, and even a few of the great-grandchildren filled every corner of the house. Maylena stood at the center of it all, greeting everyone with her signature calm and grace. She was the matriarch, the anchor of the family, and every person who entered the house seemed to gravitate toward her.

There was a moment when Alyssa stood off to the side, looking around at her family. It was hard to miss the way they all rallied around her grandmother. Luke and Tamara played with the younger kids, Uncle Marcus and Aunt Linda shared stories in the kitchen with her mom, and the older members of the family exchanged memories on the porch. It was in these small, everyday moments that Alyssa saw the ripple effect of Grandma Maylena's love and faith.

Dr. Monique Rodgers

Maylena had raised her children with the same kind of quiet faith that she now imparted to her grandchildren and great-grandchildren. It wasn't a loud, in-your-face kind of faith—it was steady, grounded in prayer and patience, and rooted in trust. She'd always taught her children that faith wasn't just something you spoke about; it was something you lived.

As the afternoon faded into evening, the family gathered around the long wooden dining table. Maylena's children and grandchildren filled the seats, while the younger ones found places on the floor, some with their plates on their laps. It felt like a picture out of time—a snapshot of unity, love, and history.

Alyssa sat beside her grandmother, her heart swelling with emotion. The room was full of laughter and chatter, but in that moment, she felt something deeper—something spiritual. Her grandmother had built this family on the foundation of love, faith, and resilience, and it was clear that the ripple effect of that foundation stretched far beyond just the immediate family.

After everyone had been served, Maylena stood up from her seat. The room grew quieter, as if everyone knew the tradition. It wasn't unusual for Grandma Maylena to say grace before a meal, but there was something about her prayers that always stopped Alyssa in her tracks.

Maylena looked around at all of her children, grandchildren, and great-grandchildren, her eyes soft with love. "Father God," she began, her voice steady but full of emotion, "we thank You for this day, for this family, and for the blessings You've given us. I ask that You continue to guide each of us, that You help us grow in faith, and that You strengthen our bonds. Thank You for this food, and thank You for the gift of family. In Jesus' name, amen."

"Amen," the room echoed.

Alyssa felt a lump in her throat as she joined in the prayer. There was something sacred about the way Maylena spoke to God—so confident, so humble, and so filled with love. As the meal was served and the family dove into their plates, Alyssa couldn't help but think about the legacy her grandmother had created. This family wasn't just connected by blood—it was connected by something much stronger.

After dinner, the conversations spilled into the living room, and people began to share their favorite memories of the past. Stories were told of Maylena's early years, of the struggles she had overcome, and of the lessons she had taught. Even the youngest of the great-grandchildren knew the stories by heart.

"Grandma Maylena," Alyssa said as they sat together on the porch after dinner, "how did you do it? How did you raise all of us with such love and faith?"

Maylena smiled softly. "I just kept trusting. I didn't have all the answers, but I had faith. I believed that God would give me the strength to get through every challenge. And when things got hard, I relied on my family, on my faith, and on God's promises."

Alyssa leaned back in her chair, taking it all in. She realized that this family gathering wasn't just about spending time together—it was about the inheritance of faith that had been passed down through generations. Maylena's love and faith had created a ripple that reached beyond just the walls of her home, extending into the hearts of everyone in her family.

Alyssa had always been proud of her family, but tonight, as she watched her grandmother laugh with her children and grandchildren, she felt a sense of awe. This was a family built on love, resilience, and unwavering faith.

And now, as the evening came to a close, Alyssa knew that her part in this legacy was just beginning. She would carry the seeds of her grandmother's faith into the world, sharing her story and her lessons, and passing them on to future generations.

In that moment, as the laughter of her family surrounded her, Alyssa understood that the ripple effect of love and faith didn't just fade away. It grew stronger with each passing year, continuing to shape and mold the future, just as it had done for generations before her.

The family gathering was more than just a reunion—it was a reminder of what truly mattered: the love of family, the strength of faith, and the power of a legacy that would never fade.

Chapter 10:

Harvest of Love

The summer days had slipped by like the gentle breeze that rustled the leaves of the old oak tree in Grandma Maylena's yard. Alyssa couldn't believe how quickly the weeks had passed. It felt as though she had just arrived, overwhelmed and disconnected from everything, and now, the thought of leaving this peaceful haven filled her with a sense of heaviness. But as she sat on the porch one last time, watching the sun set behind the hills, she realized how much she had changed.

She had come here to escape—to find peace in the chaos of her life, to reconnect with her family, and perhaps, to find her way back to her faith. And now, with her notebook full of ideas, scribbled thoughts, and chapters she'd written from her heart, Alyssa knew that her life would never be the same.

The garden, which had been a place of solace and reflection for her over the past few weeks, had become a symbol of her own personal growth. Alyssa had watched it bloom, just as she had, nourished by patience, care, and the steady hand of her grandmother. Maylena had taught her more than how to tend to the soil; she had shown her how to cultivate a life of purpose, faith, and love.

This was the last evening of the summer, and the whole family had gathered for one final meal together. The long wooden table on the porch was covered in dishes made from the garden's harvest—freshly picked tomatoes, cucumbers, collard greens, and, of course, the cornbread that Alyssa had come to love so much. The air was warm but not stifling, the sun casting a golden hue over everything, and the sounds of cicadas filled the air. It felt like the perfect way to close this chapter.

Alyssa stood beside her grandmother, who was busy setting the table, her hands moving with practiced ease, arranging the dishes just so. Despite the hustle and bustle, there was a calmness about Maylena, a quiet certainty that everything would come together in its own time.

"You've really outdone yourself, Grandma," Alyssa said, her voice thick with emotion. She watched her grandmother's hands as they carefully placed the last dish on the table, smoothing her apron as she stood back to admire her work.

"It's not about the food, child," Maylena said, her voice soft yet firm. "It's about the love that goes into it. The love that's shared. That's the real nourishment."

Alyssa took a deep breath and glanced around the table, noticing the faces of her family—the people who had shaped her, who had been there for her even when she didn't realize she needed them. Her cousins, her aunts, her uncles—all gathered here, sharing in the bounty of their labor, the fruits of their faith and patience. This meal, like everything else, was an offering of love.

They all sat down, and the conversation flowed easily, just as it always had. Her cousins joked about old family stories, her aunt and uncle reminisced about times gone by, and the kids ran around, their laughter filling the spaces between the adults' words.

Dr. Monique Rodgers

It was in moments like these that Alyssa could feel the weight of her grandmother's wisdom, the invisible threads that connected them all. Maylena had never been the type to seek attention, but everyone in the room knew that it was her love that held this family together. Alyssa had seen it in the way she moved through life—never in a hurry, always present, always offering grace.

"So, Alyssa," her cousin Luke said, taking a bite of cornbread and looking over at her with a playful smile, "I hear you've been busy this summer."

Alyssa laughed, feeling a bit shy but grateful for the opportunity to share. "Yeah," she said, twirling her fork in the mashed potatoes. "I've been working on something... a book, actually. I'm almost done with the first draft."

Her family quieted for a moment, and then Uncle Marcus raised an eyebrow. "A book, huh? That's some serious work, Alyssa. What's it about?"

Alyssa took a deep breath, her heart racing slightly as she thought about the words she had written. "It's about my summer here, with Grandma. It's about faith, family, and how you've all taught me the power of love. It's a tribute to this place, and to Grandma, really."

Maylena looked up from her plate, her eyes warm but knowing. She had always known that Alyssa had a gift with words, but she had never pushed her to use it. She simply trusted that, when the time was right, Alyssa would find her way.

"I'm proud of you, child," Maylena said softly, her voice filled with emotion. "It's a good thing to give voice to your story. Don't ever forget that."

Alyssa's eyes welled up with tears. The validation she hadn't realized she was craving flooded her chest. She had always struggled with the idea of being seen, of sharing her heart with others, but in this moment, in this place, she felt safe enough to be vulnerable.

"I think I've been running from my story for a long time," Alyssa confessed, her voice thick with emotion. "I didn't want to face it. But being here, being with all of you, has shown me that my story is important. And maybe it's not just for me—it's for others too."

Grandma Maylena smiled gently, a quiet pride in her eyes. "Your story is always for others, child. You don't know the impact you can have until you share it."

As they finished the meal, the conversation shifted to lighter topics, but Alyssa couldn't shake the weight of what her grandmother had said. There was something so powerful about the way Maylena lived her life—how she planted seeds of faith in everything she did, how she had nurtured and cultivated not just a garden, but a legacy. It wasn't just about growing food—it was about growing people, growing hearts, and growing love.

Later that evening, after the plates had been cleared and the dishes washed, Alyssa found herself alone in the garden, the last remnants of sunlight fading into the horizon. She stood by the tomato plants, their branches heavy with fruit, and closed her eyes. The evening air was warm, filled with the scent of soil and flowers, and for a moment, Alyssa let herself be completely still.

Dr. Monique Rodgers

She could feel her grandmother's presence beside her, even though Maylena wasn't physically there. Her faith, her wisdom, her love—it all surrounded her like a warm blanket, comforting her in a way she hadn't felt in years.

Alyssa took out her notebook, now nearly full with the words she had written over the past few weeks. She had poured her heart into every page, every sentence. But as she looked down at the pages, she realized that it wasn't just the words that mattered—it was the journey that had brought her here.

It was the garden. It was the meals shared around the table. It was the laughter and the tears and the quiet moments of reflection. It was the love that had been passed down through generations, and the faith that had been the foundation of it all.

She had come here looking for a way to heal, to reconnect with her faith, and to find a sense of purpose. What she had found was so much more. She had found her family, her roots, and the deep well of strength that ran through them all.

As the moon rose high in the sky, Alyssa knew that her life would be different from this point forward. She was no longer just a writer; she was a keeper of stories, a bearer of her grandmother's legacy. And as she looked down at the pages of her book, she knew that this was only the beginning.

In the silence of the garden, surrounded by the bounty of the earth and the love of her family, Alyssa made a promise to herself—and to her grandmother—that she would carry this legacy forward. She would continue to plant seeds of love and faith, just as Maylena had done before her.

And as she stood there, her heart full of gratitude and peace, Alyssa understood that the harvest of love wasn't just something to look forward to—it was something she was already living.

Epilogue:

A Legacy Blooming

Years passed, and the seasons continued their eternal cycle—spring, summer, fall, and winter. But for Alyssa Robinson, those seasons had taken on new meaning. She had returned to her bustling life as a bestselling author, the whirlwind of deadlines and book tours still a constant companion. Yet, every time the pressure mounted or the world felt too heavy, she would close her eyes and picture Grandma Maylena's garden—the rich soil, the rows of vegetables, the quiet wisdom that had flowed from her grandmother's lips like honey.

Alyssa had kept her promise. The book she had started that summer, a tribute to Maylena's unwavering faith and love, was now a reality. *Grandma's Garden* had become not just a bestseller but a source of light for countless readers. It was more than just a book—it was a living legacy, a reminder of the beauty that comes when we nurture the seeds of love, faith, and family.

But the legacy didn't stop with the book. Alyssa had embraced the lessons her grandmother had taught her, weaving them into every part of her life. She started a community initiative that helped mentor young women, guiding them to find their own paths through faith and perseverance, just as Maylena had done for her. She opened a garden in her hometown, a space where people could come together, work the soil, and share their stories—just like the summers spent at Grandma's house.

As Alyssa stood in that garden, feeling the warm embrace of the earth beneath her feet, she could almost hear Grandma's voice: *"Life is like a garden. You plant seeds, you nurture them, and you trust God will bring the harvest."*

It had been a few years since Maylena's passing. The old oak tree in the backyard had grown taller, its branches reaching toward the sky, just as the family had grown since her death. Her children, grandchildren, and great-grandchildren carried forward the traditions of faith and love she had instilled in them. The house that had once felt too quiet without her presence was now filled with new memories, new voices, and new laughter.

And though the seasons would change and life would continue to move forward, Alyssa knew one thing for certain: the garden was always there. The garden of her grandmother's love, wisdom, and faith. It lived in the soil beneath her feet, in the stories shared around the dinner table, in the hearts of every person who had been touched by Maylena's quiet, powerful legacy.

Alyssa smiled as she looked over the rows of tomatoes, cucumbers, and flowers that had grown tall in the garden she had helped start. The plants were now thriving, just as her own heart had done since that summer.

It wasn't just a harvest of food—it was a harvest of love, of faith, and of family. And it was a harvest that would continue to bloom for generations to come.

As the sun set over the garden, casting a warm glow on the plants and flowers, Alyssa whispered a silent prayer, her heart full of gratitude.

Thank you, Grandma. Your love will always grow within me.

And with that, Alyssa turned back toward her home, ready to share her grandmother's story with the world—and to keep planting seeds of love wherever she went.

Because, as Maylena had taught her, every act of kindness, every word of faith, and every moment spent with family was a seed that would grow into something beautiful.

And this was just the beginning.

About the Author

Dr. Monique Rodgers is an international bestselling author, CEO, visionary, and master business coach whose extraordinary career spans a multitude of disciplines. A certified vegan health coach, motivational speaker, entrepreneur, educator, and Mary Kay independent advanced color & skin care consultant, Dr. Rodgers is widely recognized as a literary genius and notable writing coach. She is the founder and serial entrepreneur behind several successful ventures, and her remarkable work continues to inspire and impact the lives of countless individuals worldwide.

Throughout her career, Dr. Rodgers has authored an impressive 155 books, including renowned titles such as *Hello! My Name is Millennial*, *Picking Up the Pieces*, *The Mystical Land of Twinville*, *Falling in Love with Jesus*, *Accelerate*, *Overcoming Writer's Block*, *Just Breathe*, *Called to Intercede Volumes 1-14*, and *I Am Black History*, to name just a few. Additionally, she has contributed as a co-author in collaborations like *Jumpstart Your Mind*, *Speak Up: We Deserve to Be Heard*, *Finding Joy in the Journey Volume 2*, and *Let the Kingdompreneurs Speak*.

Dr. Rodgers' exceptional work has earned her numerous

accolades and recognition, including the prestigious Presidential Lifetime Achievement Award in 2023. She is also a proud member of the KDP Scholars & Honor Society, underscoring her standing as a distinguished leader in the literary world. Dr. Rodgers has graced prominent media platforms such as *Rachel Speaks Radio Program*, *The Love Walk Podcast*, *The Glory Network*, *God's Glory Radio Show*, *The Miracle Zone*, *The Healing Zone*, *The Joyce Kiwani Adams Show*, and many others, where she shares her wisdom and insights with global audiences.

Her presence has been felt on multiple platforms, and she has served as a TV host for WATCTV. Her work has been featured in *Heart and Soul Magazine*, *My Story the Magazine*, and Kish Magazine's *Top 20 Authors of 2021*. She has also been honored with inclusion in *Marquis*

Who's Who in America 2021-2022. Beyond her literary endeavors, Dr. Rodgers is dedicated to volunteerism, having served on the executive team of *Lady Deliverers Arise,* as a board member for *Aniyah Space,* and as a member of the *I Am My Sister* organization.

A certified master business coach and health advocate, Dr. Rodgers has played key leadership roles in both the business and ministry sectors. She currently serves as an Awakening Prayer Hub leader in Raleigh, under the tutelage of Apostle Jennifer LeClaire, and as an ambassador for Kingdom Sniper Institute, mentored by Evangelist Latrice Ryan. Dr. Rodgers' academic credentials include an undergraduate degree from Oral Roberts University, a Master of Science degree, and a doctorate in global leadership from Colorado Technical

University. She has also studied at The Black Business School online.

Looking ahead, Dr. Rodgers remains committed to expanding her expertise and serving others through ministry. Her vision includes helping over one hundred authors complete and publish their books, training intercessors to deepen their relationship with God, and equipping marketplace prophets and leaders for success. Driven by her passion for empowering others, Dr. Rodgers continues to influence and inspire, using her voice and platform to bring about lasting change and positive transformation in the lives of many.

To stay connected with Dr. Monique Rodgers

Contact information:
www.getwriteoncoaching.com
www.meetdrmonique.com
Facebook: www.facebook.com/moniquerodgers2
Instagram: @drroyalty7
Twitter: @DrMonique7
LinkedIn: Dr. Monique Rodgers
YouTube: Dr. Monique Rodgers
Clubhouse: @DrMonique7
Email: calledtointerecede@gmail.com

Made in the USA
Columbia, SC
24 December 2024

48567928R00069